# Bend at Your Knees...If You Please!

## By Sharon Penchina C.Ht. & Dr. Stuart Hoffman

2 Imagine
Scottsdale, Arizona
United States of America

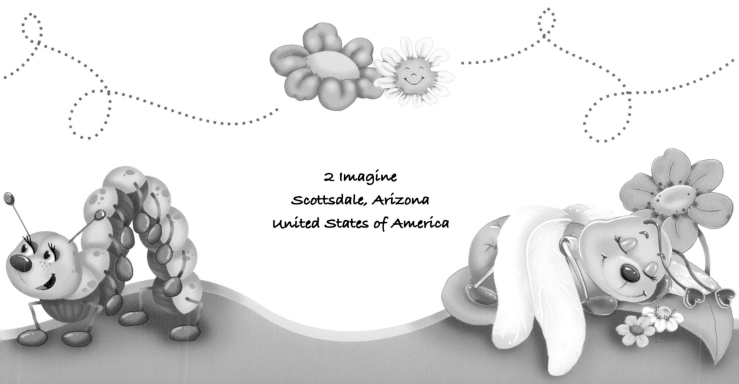

# Bend at your Knees...If You Please!

bend

Part 3 of the "I Am a Lovable ME!"
Self-EMPOWERMENT series
for children and their adults
encourages you to love, respect and
care for your body!

exercise

flow

GOOD POSTURE, EXERCISE

AND STRETCHING

WILL IMPROVE THE QUALITY OF YOUR LIFE!

stretch

# DID YOU KNOW??

- There are 30 positive affirmations in this book.

- Stretching makes your muscles long and strong.

- Stretching helps you be flexible.

- You can run, jump, and swim better when you stretch.

- Stretching prevents muscles from being hurt.

- Stretching helps relax you.

- Stretching is fun.

- Exercising gives your brain more oxygen

- Exercising your body helps it grow up strong.

- Exercise makes you feel good about yourself.

- Good posture keeps the joints in your body protected from undue wear and tear.

- Good posture allows your brain to get more oxygen.

- Good posture gives you strength and flexibility.

- Good posture reflects good health.

- Good posture makes exercise more enjoyable.

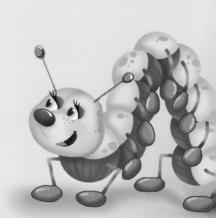

- Good posture gives you a clear mind.

- Good posture enhances your appearance, well being and self-image.

It's very important to relax; a restful sleep can be sheer delight!

I am a peaceful sleeper.

I rest throughout the night.

I am strong and I am healthy.

My body helps me throughout the day......

Lovable
❤ Me ❤

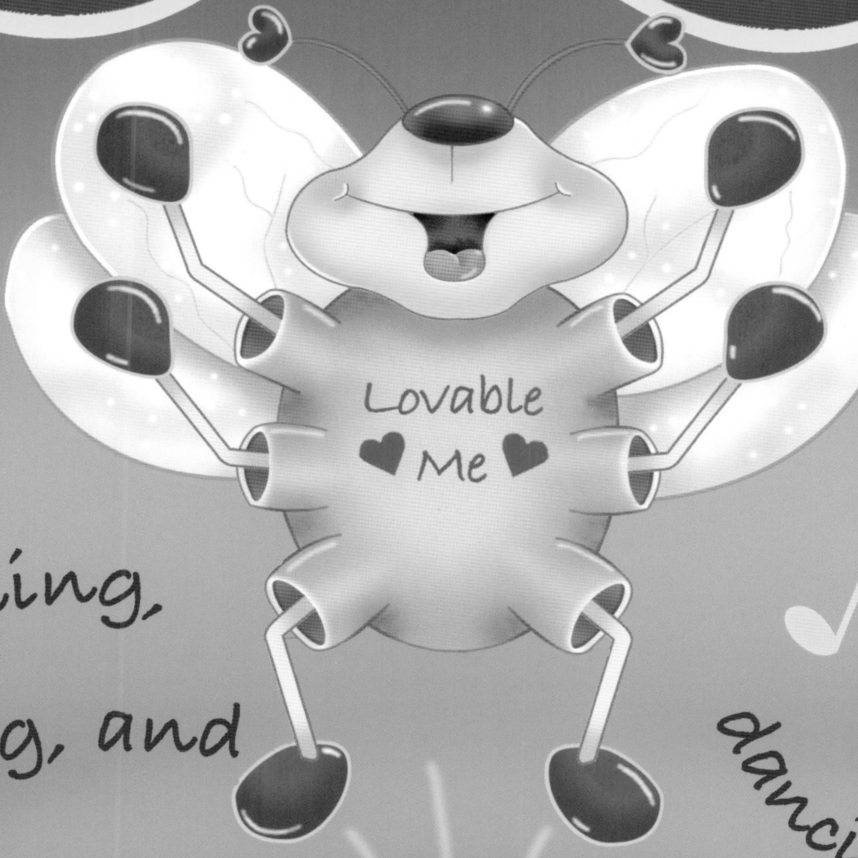


.....running,
jumping, and
dancing too,
serving me whenever I play.

I exercise quite often...

...cause it really feels so great.

...It keeps my body healthy.

I maintain a perfect weight.

I stretch my muscles and my limbs.

that keeps me rather fit.

Lovable ♥ Me ♥

I can do this while I'm standing up....

...or even when I sit.

Lovable
♥ Me ♥

I am in perfect balance;

I am as steady as I can be.

My feet are pointed straight ahead.

I'm as solid as a tree.

I am quite limber and flexible.

I move and bend and flow.

It's easy for me to get around, no matter which way I go.

I can reach up to the sky.

I respect and love my body,
as you can plainly see.

I feed my body healthy foods
and treat it lovingly.

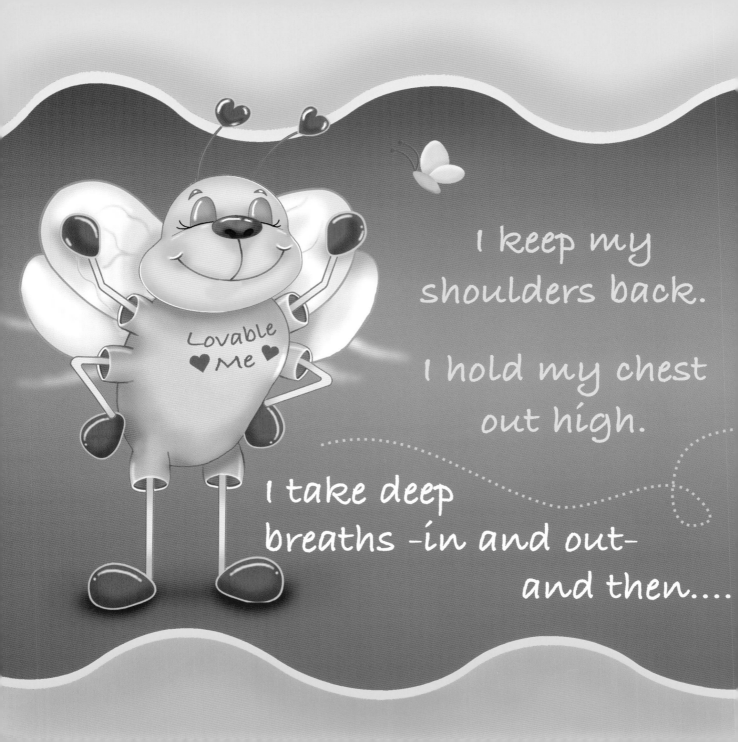

........I breathe a sigh.

Whether I am home alone,

or I sit in a crowd,

I sit up straight in my chair,

and, I'm feeling proud!